CHRISTMAS CATCH UPS

CAROLINE LEE

Dear Reader,

These stories are intended as a chance to catch up with our favorite couples. In 2017, the first four catch-ups ("catching up" with my first six RER couples) were published. All four of those stories were shaped around the theme of "motherhood," so I've left the dedication as is.
In 2018, another six came along. They're presented here as ten individual stories.

I hope you enjoy seeing your friends again!

—Caroline

ALLISON AND JOSHUA

Allison and Joshua
(*Midwife's Marvel*)

"I hate you! You're not my real mother!"

Allison's twelve-year-old daughter stomped out of the living room, and they all heard the slam of the girl's bedroom door.

When Allison glanced at her husband, Joshua, it was to see a wince he hadn't quite managed to soothe away. She kept her normal serene expression locked in place, because Colin—their eight year old—was tucked up under his dad's arm, and was looking worried enough.

The boy had had enough to be worried about in his short life, Lord knows, and his new parents had vowed he wouldn't find anything to worry about here in their home.

But now he was glancing anxiously between his sister's retreating back and Allison's face. "She didn't mean it!" he finally blurted. "She really does love you, we both do. She's just…"

Allison sighed, hating that Colin was so troubled. "She's a teenager." She shared a sad smile with Joshua. "Don't worry. Dad and I have discussed it."

The mention of "Dad" calmed Colin, as it always did. He and Joshua had a special bond, built of a mutual love of rocket ships and space and reading science fiction together. That bond had helped Colin settle into his new life much easier than his sister.

Joshua offered another gentle smile. "But it's Christmas Eve."

What he didn't say was *"Yeah, but of all the days to let her stew in her own room and wait for her to understand her feelings because she's disappointed she's not getting a smartphone like her friends...this isn't it."* He didn't have to, because Allison saw it in his eyes, and agreed.

"I'll go check on the popcorn," she called on her way out the door.

But instead of turning towards the kitchen, she headed down the hall to the bedrooms in their quaint ranch-style house. As agreed, she made sure to knock on the door of her daughter's room.

"Go away."

"Nellie, please let me in. It's Christmas Eve."

A pause. Then: *"Fine."*

Once inside the room—plastered in posters of boy bands she'd never heard of before Nellie came into her life—Allison sat on her daughter's bed and stretched a hesitant hand over the girl's hair. Nellie was lying on her stomach, her head turned towards the wall, buried in a pillow. At least she wasn't actively crying.

"Honey, I'm sorry you don't like our decision, but we're not going to change it. Your father—"

She bit down on the word. Unlike her brother, Nellie had yet to fully accept them as her parents, no matter how much they loved one another.

"Joshua and I both feel that you're too young to have a smartphone. Our decision is that if you can show us you're mature enough to handle the responsibility and rules that come with owning one, we'll consider it when you turn thirteen."

Nellie knew this—they'd been over it enough times—but maybe she'd been hoping for a Christmas miracle or something when she'd asked yet again that evening, just as they were settling in for a movie.

When she didn't respond, Allison sighed and stroked the girl's long black hair, so like her own. "You know, it's not easy suddenly becoming a mom. I've watched so many little girls being born, being handed to their mothers, seeing the look of joy on those mothers' faces... But I didn't think it would ever happen to me. I'm a midwife—it didn't occur to me that I could become a mother, without having to go through pregnancy and childbirth, and then infancy and toddlerhood and losing teeth and learning to ride bikes and all that. But suddenly I *am* a mother, to the most wonderful little girl." She sighed again. "And I'm sorry if I don't want you to grow up too fast. If I want to enjoy you being a little girl for just a little while longer, because I didn't get to love you when you were *really* little."

Nellie still didn't respond, but she did grunt a little and move her hair out of her way—without rolling over—so Allison could reach her back to rub it. Her heart lightening a little, Allison did, pleased that there was still *some*thing she could do correctly.

"When we stood in front of that judge, Joshua and I promised to love and respect you. But we asked the same from you. You promised to love and respect us, like a family should."

Finally, Nellie rolled over, and buried her face in Allison's side. "I *do* love you." Her words were muffled. "Please don't send me away."

Allison's heart clenched. "Oh, honey." She leaned over as well as she could to awkwardly wrap her arms around the girl. "You're my *daughter*. I could never send you away! All mothers and daughters fight sometimes, and I remember how rough it is being a teenaged girl." She squeezed extra tight. "I love you, and I want you to know that whatever happens in the coming years—no matter how many fights we get into over smartphones or boyfriends or makeup or whatever—I'm always going to love you. And respect you."

Sniffing, Nellie raised her head, and Allison was pleased to see she wasn't crying. Still, the girl's smile was a little watery when she teased, "Boyfriends? Eww."

Allison tightened her hold on her little girl. "Can I get that in writing? You know, for in a few years?"

"Knock-knock!" came the call from the doorway.

"*Daaaad,*" Colin moaned. "You're not supposed to *say* 'knock-knock.' Just *knock!*"

"The door was open," Joshua mock-whispered to the boy. "I thought it would be weird to knock."

"*You're* weird," Colin retorted.

Nellie rolled her eyes. "What is this, a party?"

Her brother grinned and took that as an invitation to enter, running across the room and jumping onto the bed. Unfortunately, he landed on top of his sister, who let out a big *whuff,* but didn't shove the boy off. Instead, she leaned and twisted enough to wrap her arm around her brother and squeeze him. The fact that the two kids were really affectionate with each other always made Allison smile, and tonight was no exception.

Joshua followed the boy across the room, and perched beside Allison on the edge of the bed. He reached over to take her hand, his brown eyes behind his glasses silently asking if everything was alright. Still smiling, Allison nodded and tightened her grip on his fingers.

Parenting wasn't easy—especially not when it came to teenaged girls—but Allison was blessed beyond measure when she'd teamed up with Joshua for this adventure. Last Christmas she never would've thought she'd be spending this year's holiday with her two children and her husband—the loves of her life.

Joshua lifted Allison's hand to his lips. "Merry Christmas, sweetheart."

"Merry Christmas, Mom and Dad," Colin quipped from his position, half-laying on his sister with his neck in a headlock.

"Merry Christmas, honey. I love you all very much," she replied, wondering if his sister would ever show as much affection to her new parents.

But Nellie gave her the best present of all. The girl's smile was still a little wobbly when she looked up at Allison with eyes so like her own, and said the word Allison had been hoping to hear.

"I love you too, Mom."

CHARLEY AND TRISTAN

Charley and Tristan
(*Trusting Tristan*)

"You planning on calling your Dad or Bradley tonight?" Tristan asked as they left the church with the rest of the crowd, on the way to the ranch's tree-lighting ceremony.

The question startled Charley so much she stopped walking, but quickly recovered and shook her head. "No, and I can't imagine they're expecting it." *Christmas dinner tomorrow will be bad enough.* "We don't really have Christmas Eve traditions, you know?"

Her fiancé grunted, but took her hand in his. She was glad for his warmth as the December air filled her lungs. *This* was the nicest Christmas Eve tradition she could imagine; in her pocket she held the ornaments she and Tristan had just exchanged, and they'd wait their turn to hang them on the ancient tree in the center of the ranch. Here at River's End Ranch, she was connected to something, she *belonged*. She had a family who accepted and loved her.

Just like Tristan.

Speaking of family… "Have you considered calling your father tomorrow?" she hesitantly asked.

Beside her, she felt him shrug.

"Been thinking about it, actually."

"Really?"

With Tristan's dad in prison, he hadn't spoken to the man in years. And after what his family had done to him, Charley didn't blame him, and would never push him. Still, this was the season for forgiveness, and all that.

"Yeah." He smiled crookedly. "But I'm not sure yet."

She nodded knowingly. "I get it." Neither of them had a healthy relationship with their fathers.

Maybe he was thinking along the same lines, because later, when they were watching the guests chatting and waiting their turns around the tree, Tristan said, "You know, if you and I ever have kids, I swear I'm going to be a better father than ours were to us. I'm going to teach them how to make good choices, and then I'm going to let them make those choices on their own. I'm not going to push my beliefs on them, or force them to follow my footsteps. I'm not—what?"

He must've just noticed her standing there with her mouth open. Charley snapped it closed, then shook herself again. "Nothing. It's just—" *Wow.* "This is the first time you've ever mentioned wanting to have kids. With me, I mean."

It was his turn to look uncomfortable. "Oh." His hands were jammed in the pockets of his leather coat now, and he looked at the ground. "Sorry. But..." His gaze flicked up to hers, then away. "But it's true. I want to be a dad someday. I mean, if you're up for it."

Wow. Charley wasn't sure how to answer him. Wasn't sure how to explain...

"That is, assuming you want kids."

Nothing for it, but to jump right in. "I don't know." She shrugged. "I don't *dislike* kids, but I just don't think..." Another shrug. "I'm not real feminine, you know?" She scuffed her black steel-toed boots in the packed snow. "I don't know anything about being a mom. I can't imagine I'd make a very good one."

Tristan startled a squeak out of her when he grabbed her shoulders and twisted her to face him.

"You're a total warrior, Charley, but that doesn't mean you're not a woman."

He kissed her, as if he was proving a point, but she didn't mind one bit. His kisses always made her toes curl.

"You're an incredible woman, and you're going to make an incredible mother, if you want to be." Lightly, he traced the back of one gloved finger down her cheek. "Mothering isn't something everyone's born to do, and nobody gets a manual, but you're smart and capable and totally amazing. You'd be great at it, even if we were totally making it up as we went along."

He always knew exactly what to say, didn't he? Charley smiled shyly up at him, not caring at all that their breaths were frosting in the cold air, or that they were surrounded by a hundred guests.

"I love you, Tristan."

"I love you too, Charley. Merry Christmas."

She cleared her throat. "So, kids, huh? That seems…sudden."

His arms wrapped around her. "I dunno. Christmas seemed like a good time to bring it up."

"It's just…most couples get married first."

He stiffened, and she hid her wince. They'd been unofficially engaged since the summer, and not once had either brought up the "M" word. Tristan was still settling into normal life; once his arm had healed, he'd taken on more hours at the ranch, and was able to afford an apartment in town. They were together all the time, but it wasn't like being married. At least, she had to assume, based on her observations of all the married couples around here…

"Sorry, Charley." Tristan sighed. "I didn't want to push you."

What? "You didn't want to push *me*? *You're* the one who's been totally reinventing himself!"

He shrugged. "Yeah, but I'm still…you know." His hold loosened, and he looked away. "I'm just an ex-con, and you're…"

Suddenly, it all clicked. "*This again?*" She stepped back and jabbed a finger in his chest. "This is about you thinking you're not worthy enough, isn't it? Well, that's *stupid*, Tristan Quarles! I would think after the last few months, you would've gotten in through your thick head. I *love* you. I *want* to be married to you. I would be *lucky* to be married to you! This whole 'you not being worthy' thing is the *dumbest*—"

She bit her words off when his hand wrapped around her finger, and his other pulled her closer again.

"You sure about that, Charley?" he asked softly, staring down at her with those gorgeous hazel eyes. "You *want* to be married to me?"

"I proposed to *you*, remember?"

"Well, alright then." He nodded slowly, and his lips curved into a smile. "How about Tuesday?"

"Tuesday?"

"Marry me on Tuesday. We can tell your dad and Bradley about it tomorrow, and give them a stroke. Then we can call *my* dad out of the blue and tell him I'm marrying a cop—"

"*Ex*-cop."

"—then we go to the courthouse on Tuesday and get married."

Charley pretended to consider it. "*Hmmm.* Will you take me on a honeymoon next weekend?"

He chuckled. "*You* can take *me* on a honeymoon, sweetheart."

"Deal!"

And when he kissed her, the lights on the tree behind them lit up. The crowd cheered, but Charley was already cheering wildly inside. Soon she'd be a wife…

And maybe, someday, if she *wanted*…a mother.

Sadie and Shawn
(*Sarsaparilla Showdown*)

"Are we gonna open a present tonight, like we did last year? Can we, Mommy?"

Sadie smiled down at her daughter—her *step*-daughter, really, but sometimes it was hard to remember sweet Violet had only been a part of her life for a little over a year. She'd met the nine-year-old and her delicious father last fall, and now it seemed Violet remembered their first Christmas together just as well as Sadie did.

She opened her mouth to agree to the tradition, when a pair of arms wrapping around her middle interrupted her.

"You think a Christmas Eve present is a good idea, huh, Sprout?" Shawn squeezed a gently. "What do you say, *Mommy*?"

It was hard not to giggle in joy at the subtle reminder, or at the way her husband's touch still managed to make her feel.

Sadie put down the bowl of cookie dough she'd been mixing, and turned slightly in Shawn's hold to smile up at him. His hair was still slightly too long, and he still sported a short beard, but there was a light in his eyes and a spring in his step which hadn't been there a year ago.

"Hmmmm. I think we could manage that." Stretching on her tiptoes—she was short and plump and about to get plumper—Sadie offered her husband a kiss.

"*Gak!*"

From the other side of the small apartment's kitchen. Violet made the retching noises she did whenever her parents kissed in front of her, and Shawn pulled away with a laugh. Releasing Sadie, he lunged for his daughter, and lifted her squealing into the air.

"*Ho, ho, ho!*" He threw the girl over his shoulder like a sack of toys, and lowered his voice comically. "I've got a special delivery here." He swung around to face Sadie, nearly smacking his daughter—who was still giggling helplessly—into the fridge. "Do you know anyone who's been a good girl?"

Sadie pushed aside the cookie dough and pretended to think while she untied her apron. "I *guess* I've been a good girl. But good enough for a Violet? Do you think I deserve a present that special?"

From atop her father's shoulders, Violet made a noise somewhere between exasperation and laughter. "*No one* is good enough to deserve me! I'm *awesome!*"

Shawn swatted her rear end playfully. "And so modest!"

All three of them were laughing when Sadie herded her family into the small living room. They'd moved into her one-bedroom apartment—after selling Shawn's RV— last year and had been discussing the feasibility of moving into a larger one in the same complex. Since the summer camps at River's End Ranch—which Shawn had been in charge of putting together and running—had been so successful, and since the new carousel had brought in so much more business to her ice cream and coffee shop, they could afford to move. Besides, they would need the extra space.

Still, if this was going to be their last Christmas in this cozy little apartment, Sadie wanted it to be special. And that included the Christmas Eve tradition of opening one present—something she'd done as a child, and which Violet had enthusiastically embraced.

"Shawn," she began sternly, "Put my daughter down carefully, please. Santa is watching, after all."

"Yeah, Dad!" Violet snorted with laughter. "Santa's checking his list!"

The two people who held Sadie's heart collapsed onto the sofa. She was smiling when she pulled out the two special presents she'd set aside for Violet under the tree, and presented them to her daughter.

"Open the flat one first," Sadie instructed.

A huge smile of anticipation on her face, Violet tore into the box. "New PJs! Thank you!"

"What else is in there?" Shawn prompted.

"Popcorn…and hot cocoa mix?" The little girl held up the two envelopes in confusion.

Sadie nodded to the box. "They're for tonight, and our new tradition."

"A movie!" Violet pulled out the last gift, a DVD. "*Eloise at Christmastime*," she read.

"That's my all-time favorite Christmas movie," Sadie said as she joined her little family on the sofa. "I'd love to share it with you tonight."

"Isn't it a book too? I thought I saw Mrs. Shulman checking in an *Eloise* book a few months ago."

"I think you're right. We should check the catalog—maybe we could read them together!"

Violet grinned. "Cool!"

"Ahem," Shawn cleared his throat. "Before my two favorite ladies start nerding out over their books, I have a present for Violet."

Sadie elbowed him playfully. "*We* have a present."

He caught her hand and brought it to his lips. "*We* have a present."

"*Gah*, you're not going to start kissing again, are you?"

Ignoring his daughter for a moment, Shawn raised his brow at Sadie. "'Gah'? She gets that from you, you know."

Sadie stuck her tongue out at her husband, and dropped the last present onto Violet's lap.

The little girl ripped the tissue paper out of the gift bag, then grabbed a handful of material and pulled it out. "More PJs?" she asked, confused.

"Check it out, Sprout," Shawn prompted.

Violet held up the pink T-shirt, and Sadie saw the moment the girl read and understood the words printed in glitter across the chest.

"*World's Best Big Sister*?" Violet read in a whisper, her eyes round when they met her parents'. "Does this mean what I think it means?"

When Shawn nodded, Violet squealed and threw herself into their laps, and Sadie closed her eyes and inhaled her daughter's precious joy. Because as much as this hug meant to her, she didn't think she'd *ever* forget the look of absolute wonder that she'd seen on Violet's face a moment before.

They'd been so worried how Violet would react to the news. Well, actually, Shawn had insisted Violet was mature enough to be excited about the idea of a baby sister or brother, but Sadie had been more nervous. Add to that the terrible morning sickness of the last month that had prevented her from experimenting with new ice cream flavors, and she'd been just one big bundle of nerves.

"Can I have a baby sister, please?" Violet was asking, her voice muffled against her father's chest.

Shawn chuckled, and wrapped his free arm around Sadie. "I don't think we can take orders, Sprout. The baby's in there already, and we'll get to find out soon enough. Mommy's got an appointment for the blood work next week, and we thought we'd see if you wanted to go, since school is out."

Her little nose wrinkled. "Bloodwork? I dunno, sounds yucky. But I can go and hold your hand, if you'd like."

"I'd like that a lot, Sprout." Sadie smiled fondly. "But only if you want to. If you do, you're welcome to come look at some pictures of the baby too."

Violet lifted her feet into Sadie's lap, so they were all squished together. It might not be possible to sit like this for much longer, but for now, Sadie cherished the moment.

"*Hmmm*," the little girl hummed thoughtfully. "Pictures, huh? Are there any books I could read on the subject?"

Sadie burst into laughter, thinking about the way she'd rushed out to buy three different books on fetal development when she'd found out she was pregnant. "There are! We could read those together, too."

"Promise?"

Her daughter's seriousness sobered Sadie as suddenly as the laughter had burst forth. "I promise, Sprout. What's wrong?"

"Things are going to change, aren't they?"

Shawn's arms tightened around both of them. "They are. We're talking about moving into a bigger apartment upstairs. And we'll all have different jobs, different roles in our family. And our schedules might have to change, as we each help out with the baby. But we're still going to love each other just as much, because we're a team."

When he dropped a kiss to his daughter's head, Violet's eyes met Sadie's. "Promise, Mommy?"

And the tears in Sadie's eyes were partly from joy, partly from the realization Violet was growing up. "Pinky promise."

Violet nodded, and her smile bloomed again. "Merry Christmas, Mommy."

"Merry Christmas, my loves."

THE REDFERNS

The Redferns
Ellie and Will (*Whitewater Wooing*)
Dink and Jace (*Wild West Wedding*)
Belle and Elf (*Blacksmith's Beauty*)

The sound of laughter was coming from the kitchen when Ellie and Will returned from their walk. They'd used Indy needing exercise as an excuse to get out of the house, but really, any chance to spend some time together alone—Indy didn't count—was to be cherished.

Since little Reddy's birth back in August, Ellie could feel her relationship with her husband changing. Not in a bad way, just *different.* They were each no longer the most important person in the other's life, and she found herself snapping at him when she was tired or hungry or stressed. Muz assured her it was natural, and something all couples went through when they began having kids. The trick, she said, was to make sure her partner really was that: a partner on the same team.

Because even though Ellie and Will's relationship had shifted, they were still very much in love. Ellie knew there was no one she'd rather spend her life with, and she cherished these moments she got to spend alone with him, breathing in the pure, crisp Idaho air she'd fallen in love with thanks to him.

Luckily, they were surrounded by about a million family members who were always willing to give them the chance to be alone. The extended Weston clan could always be counted on to watch little Reddy—Wade's namesake, actually—and he really seemed to adore being around his cousins, who were only a few months older than him. On Ellie's side of the family, Reddy was the first grandchild—hence the one to carry her maiden name of Redfern—and thus was doted upon shamelessly. With Ellie's little sister and older brother both marrying and settling at River's End Ranch, Muz and Dad had moved to Riston as well.

And today, December 24th, they were all gathered in Ellie and Will's home.

They stopped in the foyer for a kiss, and Ellie leaned against her husband's chest, listening to the sound of his heart and their son's laughter from the kitchen. "I suppose I should go see what they're up to."

"Hmmm," Will agreed. "And I left Jace and your father in the living room debating the possible long-term benefits of investing in graham crackers."

"Really?"

"Jace called it a mental exercise, but I think Dad was being serious."

"And whose side was Elf on?"

"He was watching college football on TV, and occasionally chiming in with a vote for Nilla Wafers."

Ellie snorted. "I can see why you wanted to get out of there."

"No." Will dropped a kiss on her hair. "I wanted to get out of there so I could spend some time with my wife. But now I am energized and recharged, and I can face the cookie-investment debate."

Ellie stepped back, and nodded seriously. "Godspeed, brave warrior. You risk much."

She pretended to lay a benediction on his head, but he grabbed her around the waist for one more quick, laughing, kiss.

That's why she was still smiling when she entered the kitchen to see Muz holding the baby, and Dink and Belle rolling out cookie dough. Her sister looked up and smiled knowingly.

"You look happy! I guess the winter air agrees with you, huh?" she teased.

"Winter air?" Belle threw in, not looking up from her choice of cookie cutters. "I'd say it's more like a certain *man* agreed with her."

Dink jabbed her sister-in-law with an elbow. "Oh, like you have room to talk? I saw you sitting on my big brother's lap earlier, when you went in there to let them 'test' the last batch of cookies."

Belle gasped in mock-indignation. "*He* pulled *me* down, I'll have you know. I am *nothing* if not professional when it comes to Peanut Butter Kisses."

"The cookie or the actual kiss?"

Ellie was glad when Muz interrupted their banter, worried it might come back around to her again, and not knowing if she needed to defend herself against the kissing-in-the-snow allegations.

"My little Schnoogle-Bottom here prefers his kisses peanut-free, don't you, my love?" Muz blew a raspberry on the baby's Christmas-onesie-encased tummy. "Because he thrives on kisses, yes he does."

Reddy's laughter was high-pitched, and never failed to make Ellie smile. He'd only recently started laughing so much, and his NanaMuz was one of his favorite people. Probably because of her ridiculous made-up nicknames.

"I suppose 'Schnoogle-Bottom' is better than 'Pumpernickel-Melon' or whatever it was you were calling him last week," Belle said as she pressed the cookie cutters into the dough. "I dunno where you come up with this stuff, Muz."

Ellie crossed to get a root beer from the fridge. "You don't need to worry about it 'til it starts making sense."

"All of my words make perfect sense, yes they do," Muz said to the baby. "Don't they, Schmoopy?"

"Is there a reason all of her words start with 'schmoo?'" Belle asked Dink in a mock-whisper.

"Not *all* of them," Dink replied. "She calls my brother 'Elfikins', and Dad used to be 'Canoodle.'"

Ellie remembered that one. "Actually," she corrected. "I think it was 'Little Baby Canoodle-Puff,' wasn't it?"

While Belle hid her snort of laughter, Muz blew another raspberry on Reddy's tummy. "See? They all make perfect sense, don't they? Don't you think Papa is a Canoodle-Puff, my little Schnookle-Bottom?"

The baby chose that moment to let out a sweet little fart, which sent his adoring ladies—even Ellie—into peals of laughter.

"I think—" Belle tried to choke out between chuckles, "I think you should call him 'Cutie-Poots'. No, wait!" She straightened, still holding her stomach. "I call that! That's my nickname for him! Cutie-Poots, you can't have that, I copyright it!"

Ellie put back the root beer, unopened, knowing she was laughing too hard to try to drink anything carbonated. "I dunno, I might have to steal it…"

Muz had Reddy up against her shoulder and was patting his back while giving the younger women a haughty glare. "Don't be ridiculous. 'Cutie-Poots' is a terrible nickname."

Belle could tease her mother-in-law with the rest of them. "Oh, but Schnoogie isn't?"

"*Schnoogle-Bottom*, thankyouverymuch," Muz said, her nose in the air. "Now, if you don't mind, I'm going to take little Schnooklerino here up to his room for a new diaper and some NanaMuz time."

As she walked by, she held out the baby for Ellie to kiss. That baby-head smell would never get old, and Ellie took a big whiff, closing her eyes in bliss.

"Okay, Muz, but try not to teach him any nonsense. Will wants his first word to be 'Dada.'"

"*Nonsense?*" Muz said to the baby as she headed for the stairs, pretending to be offended. "Nonsense. Did you hear that, Schnookikins? She thinks I'm nonsensical…"

If Ellie hadn't been looking at her sister right as Muz walked out the door, she would have missed the wistful look that floated across Dink's face. Why? Because of the women's easy banter, or because of the baby?

Come to think of it, Dink and Jace had been married just as long as Ellie and Will had. They both adored kids, and were instrumental in the success of the new kids' camp last summer. Was it because they were still living in that tiny house they hadn't had kids yet?

And for that matter, when was Belle going to get around to having a baby? Sure, she and Ellie's brother had been married less than a year, but there's no time like the present... Ellie told herself to stop trying to manage everyone else's lives.

It was just... She and Will were so happy with little Reddy in their lives. She wanted everyone to experience that happiness. The happiness that came from looking into the eyes of your baby son or daughter and knowing a love that you could never before have imagined. It was just so special, and she wanted her sister and brother to experience that too.

Yep, time to meddle.

"Soooo, Belle..." Ellie stepped up to the other side of the kitchen island and began scooping the cut cookies up off the counter with the spatula and sliding them onto the prepared trays. "Have you and Elf thought about having a baby?"

"Having a baby?" snorted Belle, without looking up from her careful cookie-cutter placement. "Is that what the kids are calling it these days? I *am* a married woman, no need to get euphemistic."

"Eeew!" Ellie squealed. "I don't need to think of my big brother *making babies*!"

The three of them giggled a little before Belle looked up, one brow raised.

"Oh, you were being serious? No. No *no no*!" She held up a metal Santa in one hand and a reindeer in the other. "I'm only twenty-four, and I get to cuddle all the babies I want to at work, when I have to cover for Debbie in the infants' room. Elf and I have talked about it..." She shrugged, and reached for a third cookie cutter. "But we both agree that *if* we want kids, it won't be for a while yet. I'm happy with my job, especially now that it's winter and I get to help on the bunny slopes with the youngest skiers. And Elf and I..." She blushed slightly, no longer meeting Ellie's eyes. "Well, we're pretty happy right now, it being just the two of us."

Hmmm. Well, it was hard to fault her reasoning. Belle was a few years younger than her sisters-in-law, and Ellie could see how she might not be ready for kids yet. It was that "if" that concerned her. How could Belle not want kids? Especially since she was so good with them? Ellie figured it was up to her to convince Belle otherwise... Luckily, she had a few years.

Meanwhile... Ellie turned to her sister, who had been doing her best to ignore the conversation, head bent industriously over the dough she was rolling out for Belle's cutters.

"How about you, Dink? I'll bet you and Jace would make *the* most beautiful babies. My Reddy needs a cousin to play with! How about it?"

Without looking up from her work, Dink replied, "How about what?"

"Babies!" The word burst out of Ellie in an exasperated huff. "When are you and Jace going to start having kids?"

"Oh." Dink seem to be paying special attention to one particular corner of the rolled dough, going over it again and again with the pin. Finally she shrugged. "Not yet."

There was something about the way she answered, about the way she seemed to want to avoid the conversation, which had Ellie's sisterly instincts on the rise.

"Not yet? As in…you talked about it but decided to wait, like Belle? Or not yet, like you don't want kids? Or not yet like…?"

She trailed off, inviting Dink to explain. A long, awkward silence passed before Belle finally nudged Dink with her elbow.

"You've got to tell her," she said in a soft voice.

"Tell me what?"

Ellie's eyes darted between the two of them, wondering what Belle knew that she didn't. Neither of them looked her way, but Dink finally raised her eyes to meet Belle's.

"If you don't," Belle nodded seriously at Ellie's sister, "I will."

Part of Ellie bristled at the realization her sister-in-law and her sister had been sharing secrets behind her back. But another part of her acknowledged she had been fairly wrapped up in preparing for Reddy's arrival, and then falling in love with her baby... She supposed it was possible she hadn't spared her sister the attention she needed over the last year.

Ellie wasn't sure what to say, how to acknowledge the fault aloud, so she just pressed her lips together and waited for her sister to say something.

Finally, Dink met her eyes.

"Not yet..." She took a deep breath. "*Not yet* as in, the doctors say we can't have children."

Stunned, Ellie's first response wasn't an elegant one. "*What*? She squeaked. "What do you mean?"

When she spoke, Dink's words were monotone, as if they'd been rehearsed. "About six months ago we went to the doctor, to ask why we weren't pregnant yet. We've been trying all the old wives' suggestions, and a bunch of other silly stuff." She didn't blush, or even crack a smile. She said the words dully, like they no longer pained her. "The doctors define infertility as trying for more than a year without getting pregnant, so Jace's insurance covered all the tests." She dropped her gaze to the rolling pin in her hands, and shrugged. "The results were pretty clear. The only way we're ever going to be able to have a baby of our own is with really expensive invasive in-vitro fertilization. And even then..." She shrugged one more time. "Nothing is guaranteed."

Ellie stood there, gaping. *Dink would never have a baby*? The thought was too terrible to bear; she dropped the spatula and wrapped her arms around her middle. How *horrible,* to think of never feeling little Reddy moving inside her, never holding him in her arms. Ellie's eyes filled with tears, imagining her life without her baby in it.

"Ellie."

When Belle snapped her name, Ellie's tear-filled eyes flew to her sister-in-law's dark ones. Belle stood close enough to Dink their arms touched, and it was obvious she was lending her support.

"Ellie," Belle began again, more gently, "Whatever it is you're about to say, *think* about it first." She cut her eyes to Dink, then back again. "Think about what's needed."

Her words were slow to penetrate, but when they did, Ellie nodded slowly, understanding dawning. Her reaction to her sister's revelation had been all about *herself,* and her own feelings. Dink didn't need to hear that, or need to hear how terrible Ellie considered her situation…

She took a breath, and met her little sister's eyes. "I'm sorry, Dink. That stinks."

Dink shrugged with a nonchalance that was obviously forced. "It's okay. We're dealing with it."

"Would a hug help?"

Her sister's smile was watery, but it was there. "A hug *always* helps."

Moving around the kitchen island, Ellie wrapped Dink in a hug. After a long moment, Dink's arms snaked tentatively around her middle.

"Why didn't you tell me?" Ellie asked against her sister's teal-dyed hair, and felt a shrug in response.

"You were so wrapped up with little Reddy, I didn't want to take away from that."

Before Ellie could respond to that—to apologize for not being there for her sister—Belle joined them in the hug, wrapping her arms around both of them. So instead, Ellie spoke to her.

"Thank you for being there for Dink. I'm really glad she felt comfortable talking to you about it."

Belle smiled slightly, her cheek pressed against Dink's shoulder. "Me too."

Another pair of arms—much larger and hairier—wrapped around all of them from the other side, and Ellie's head whipped sideways to meet her brother's eyes.

"Hi!" he said brightly, not loosening his hold. "Are we doing Christmas hugs? Is that what we're doing?"

It was hard not to snort with laughter, but Ellie managed it. "We're doing comforting hugs."

"Oh, good," he deadpanned. "I'm excellent at that."

With only a little grunt, he bent his knees and lifted all three of them off the floor—not much, but enough to make Belle squeal and Ellie squirm. When he plopped them down, their little huddle broke apart, with Ellie and Belle backing away towards the island. Dink, on the other hand, turned to offer her big brother a longer hug. Elf obliged.

Jace chose that moment to enter the kitchen as well. "Are we doing Christmas hugs? Is that a thing?" He turned to Ellie. "Do we do Christmas hugs in this family?

Ellie knew he'd grown up without a real family, without the Christmas celebrations she and her siblings had treasured. But the Redferns had happily accepted him into their fold, and he'd joined in their teasing and laughter just like Will and Belle.

Today, though, the teasing seemed bittersweet.

Ellie offered a small smile. "We do hugs *anytime* in this family."

"Ah." Jace blinked his handsome light-brown eyes and turned to his wife, who was extricating herself from Elf's hug. "You finally told her, huh?"

Dink crossed to Jace, who wrapped his arms around her middle and rested his chin on the top of her head. Elf snagged Belle, pulling her up against his side, one large arm around her shoulders. He seemed to understand what was going on, and Ellie was miffed for a moment that *she* was the last to know this important news in her sister's life.

Still, she had to admit she understood their reasoning, and the very last thing Dink and Jace needed right now was for her to get all fussy because she felt slighted. So instead, she tried for a smile.

"So what are you two thinking?"

One of Jace's elegant brows rose. "In general? About hugs, or Christmas, or what?"

"About…" Ellie swallowed. "About the whole infertility thing."

"Ah." His arms tightened around Dink. "Well, we trust the doctors, so we've accepted their verdict."

Ellie met her sister's eyes, and saw that was true. And somehow, the pit in her stomach felt a little less horrible. Knowing Dink wasn't denying the tests' results, wasn't railing against the universe, disbelieving…somehow, that made it seem better.

Jace continued. "And no matter how much we loved being a part of Reddy's birth and his early weeks, we know that's not the only way to have children."

Dink nodded, bumping her head against her husband's chin. "We're not sure yet if we're totally ready for kids." She exchanged a glance with Belle, who'd said the same thing. "But we've already started looking into the fostering requirements for Idaho." She patted Jace's arms where they rested against her stomach. For the first time since her confession, she seemed animated at the topic. "Jace's experience in the foster care system showed us there are kids—babies—out there who need our love. Maybe one day we'll do IVF, but I think it's important to both of us to give a loving home to kids who have already been born."

Ellie couldn't swallow past the lump in her throat. Dink's statement had been the most beautiful thing she could recall her sister ever saying, and the pit in her stomach turned into a million tiny butterflies, who all took flight at once.

Looking at her sister, in the arms of a man who obviously loved her, Ellie knew she'd be alright. They'd *all* be alright, no matter what path to motherhood—*Or not*, she thought, glancing at Belle—the universe took them on.

This time, the tears in her eyes were from happiness. The future wasn't always what she expected, but as long as she had the love of her family, and her husband, it was beautiful. Speaking of whom…

"What'd I miss? I can only talk about Oreos and Gingersnaps for so long before I— Why are we all standing around looking emotional?"

Will came up behind Ellie and slung his arm over her shoulder as he asked the question.

She snaked her arms around his middle, and pressed her cheek against his chest, reveling in the steady beat of his heart and the certainty of his love. "We're just here, thinking about how very blessed we've been."

"Yep," Will quipped, "I *am* pretty awesome."

"Not with *you*," she snapped as she swatted his side, but then rubbed the sting out. "We're blessed because we have each other, no matter what. And because it's Christmastime."

"And because," Jace spoke up, "we have a future together."

Elf smiled down at Belle. "And no matter what, we'll have a family that suits us."

There. That's what life was all about, wasn't it?

Ellie smiled up at her husband, the man who made her a mother. "Merry Christmas."

"Merry Christmas."

JACKIE AND COOPER

Jackie and Cooper
Stepdad Surprise

From the other room, the squeal of eighteen-month-old Kalli Jo made Jackie wince slightly, but Cooper's arms tightened around her and he nuzzled her ear.

"She's fine. That stoic brother-in-law of mine brought his latest litter, that's why she's so happy."

Sure enough, the little girl soon began chanting, "Puppy! Puppy!"

Jackie grinned and wrapped her arms around her husband's neck. "I'll bet that's going to make for some adorable photos, especially with her in her pretty dress for the Christmas Eve service."

Cooper's grin was still just as heart-meltingly gorgeous as the day she'd fallen in love with him. "Why do you think I asked him to bring the little fuzzballs?"

"You think of everything," she murmured, pushing herself up on her toes to brush her lips across his.

There in the kitchen of his parents' home, she showed him how much he meant to her. When they pulled apart, Cooper pressed her head against his chest and hugged her. She sighed, content to let him hold her—and hold him in return—knowing their daughter was safe and sound in the other room with the rest of their family.

Between his job with the construction company—although since the snows started, they'd been mainly working on the interiors of the buildings the television crew needed—and hers at the spa, it was rare to find time for just the two of them. Kalli was always with them, and although Jackie adored knowing how close of a family they'd all become, she treasured the time alone with her husband.

"Thank you for setting all this up." She sighed against his chest. "I know Kalli loves seeing your family, and the puppies will be an added bonus."

He grunted softly. "I just hope Mom doesn't mind the excitement."

"I'm sure she won't."

In the months since Jackie had met Susan Weston for the first time—when she gave Cooper her wedding ring for him to give to Jackie—she'd fallen in love with this family.

It was impossible not to love Cooper's younger sister Marybeth, who was a real sweetheart. She and her husband Mack ran a kennel and boarding business on the ranch, as well as bred champion sled dogs. Cooper's twin brother Kenneth was the more serious of the two, but he was determined to become Kalli's favorite uncle—that was him singing nonsense songs to her in the other room now.

And Jackie's father-in-law Wilfred was devoted to his granddaughter. It had meant so much to Jackie, how this family had opened up their hearts and homes to her and her daughter when she'd married Cooper. She still didn't believe she deserved this much happiness, and sometimes needed to pinch herself.

Against her cheek, Cooper's chest rumbled slightly. "That was a good sermon tonight."

She hummed in agreement. "I always like the way he's talking right to us. I thought it was really special, thinking about birth and rebirth and salvation and stuff."

They'd attended Pastor Kevin's Christmas Eve service and the tree-lighting right after, but had left before everyone started exchanging ornaments, in order to get to his parents' house in time for dinner. Marybeth had been cooking all day.

"Yeah…" Cooper squeezed her a little. "It's an important reminder."

With his mom's health getting steadily worse over the last months, it was impossible *not* to think about that sort of stuff. But it was as if her three children—because of course Tripp wasn't there anymore—and their spouses had made a point to ensure his mom's last few months were going to be *special*. They were all as full of joy and light and laughter as they could be, even if it ate them up inside to see her so near the end of her life.

And Jackie would know; she'd held Cooper often enough as he'd mourned.

That was why her throat was a little thick when she squeezed him as well. "I love you, Cooper," she whispered.

He dropped a kiss on her hair. "Not as much as I love you. Thank you for bringing me everything I never knew I needed."

"Thank *you* for sharing your family with me. They mean the world to me, I hope you know."

She could *hear* his smile; that's how well she knew this man.

"I do. And I hope *you* know how much you mean to them. Having you and Kalli Jo has meant a lot to my parents, and I think Marybeth appreciates not having to answer the when-are-you-having-babies question more than once a month!"

Jackie chuckled. "And Kenneth?"

Blowing out a snort of laughter, Cooper shrugged. "Who *knows*, when it comes to that knuckleheaded brother of mine? He's probably too busy sorting his fortune to worry about *emotions*. Are you sure you fell in love with the right Weston twin? He's the richer one."

"Yeah…" she drawled out her agreement, just to irritate her husband. "But *you're* the better-looking one."

"And the smarter one. And the funnier one."

"And the humbler one," she teased.

When he lifted her off her feet, she squealed as loudly as her daughter, but turned it into a hum of appreciation as he kissed her.

Too few heartbeats later, he pressed his forehead to hers. "Well, Mrs.

Weston, shall we go rescue our wayward daughter from the clutches of those puppies."

She'd probably never get tired of hearing him call Kalli Jo "our daughter." So she smiled.

"You might be right, husband. We can only take so much Christmas cheer."

"Impossible, my love!" He tugged her towards the other room, where Kalli and Kenneth were singing together. "Merry Christmas!"

MARYBETH AND MACK

Marybeth and Mack
Yukon Yuletide

Marybeth was toasty warm under her husband's arm. Mack wasn't paying any attention to her, but that was okay. His watchful eye was keeping a sharp look-out on the two pups he'd brought to play with little Kalli. They were precious at this age, but he'd begun training them to voice commands last month with their sire Rudolph, so Mack was also using this as a chance to make sure they'd follow directions.

So far they'd done a great job of obeying when he told them "down" or "halt"… better than their niece at least. But the little one seemed to be having the time of her life, running between her uncle Kenneth and the two balls of fluff wrestling in front of the fireplace.

On Marybeth's other side, her mother made a noise like a breathy huff. Marybeth turned and took the weak hand lying limply on the chair's arm.

"She sure is cute, isn't she, Mom?" she asked gently, having understood her mother's way of laughing.

It took a few seconds for Susan Weston to turn her head—even that effort seemed to exhaust her—to face Marybeth. Her smile was slight, but it lit up Marybeth's heart to see it.

She blinked away tears, not wanting Mom to know how heart-breaking it was to see her like this. She'd been fighting so many different diseases for so long, and the whole family knew there wasn't any hope for a recovery.

This would be Marybeth's last Christmas with her Mom—with her complete family—and she was determined to make it beautiful. All of them had gathered in their childhood home, just like old times, and were celebrating with all their old traditions. Marybeth had it on authority Santa would be laying beautifully wrapped presents under the tree tonight —thanks to Kenneth—and Mack had already volunteered to make his famous French toast tomorrow morning.

This Christmas celebration was going to be as close to perfect as Marybeth could manage, so they'd have beautiful memories of Mom's last Christmas.

"I love you," she whispered to her mother.

Without her voice, Mom's only way of acknowledging and agreeing was the slight pressure on her fingers, but it was enough.

From the other armchair, Dad's laugh was booming. He was in the best of health, as always, and was doing his best to make his wife's last months comfortable. It was uncanny how well he understood Mom's thoughts and desires, and could express them for her.

"I'm just glad one of you got around to giving us grandchildren!"

Coop was in the kitchen, finishing up the dishes, but Jackie smiled happily from her place on the couch. "We've been so blessed to be a part of this family!"

Dad flashed a look at Marybeth. "We love each of you, but could always go for some more babies!"

Without looking away from the pups, Mack said in that stoic tone of his, "Grandpuppies count."

When Dad snorted, Marybeth hid her smile in Mack's shoulder. He seemed to enjoy teasing her father, but he'd never admit that, of course. When she'd met him—last Christmas—he was such an old grumpy grinch. But they'd been stuck together in a small cabin throughout a blizzard, and by the time it was done, she'd known he was a kind and gentle man with a tortured past. Together, they'd helped one another heal, and were both so much stronger because of their love.

And one of the things they were both very much in agreement about was they didn't need kids right away. It was something Marybeth was sure of, especially given her battle with anxiety and Mack still going to physical therapy because of his missing leg; they weren't ready to be parents *yet*.

But every time she held her own mother's hand, every time she realized Mom wouldn't be there to hold whatever future babies *did* come along… Well, Marybeth's surety had wavered a few times.

She knew this was the right decision, to wait another year at least before having kids, but it was also heart-breaking.

Mack had pointed out her mother understood, even if she couldn't communicate, and Marybeth held fast to that knowledge as tightly as she held Mom's hand.

From his spot in front of the couch where Jackie sat—his legs splayed in front of him to catch little Kalli when she was near him—Kenneth spoke up. "If puppies count, can I get one too?"

"Not one of mine," Mack drawled, his humor as dark as ever.

Jackie nudged him with her foot. "Cooper has been bragging he beat you to it, you know."

Kenneth twisted. "Beat me to what?"

"Becoming a dad." She nodded solemnly, but the twinkle in her eye was obvious.

Marybeth's usually serious older brother just snorted. "I don't *need* to be a dad. I'm spoiling my niece. That should count."

Kenneth was the oldest of them all, although he only beat Coop by a few minutes. He'd always been the one to herd them all along, to watch out for his siblings. His "take charge" attitude had been part of what had driven away Tripp, although no one ever mentioned that. Tripp had been a wildcard, a free spirit, and chafed under Mom's rules and Kenneth's watchful eye.

But now it seemed that maybe Kenneth was loosening up a little…at least when it came to Kalli.

"Actually, about that…" Dad cleared his throat, and waited until

Kenneth was looking at him. "Your mother and I…" He glanced at his wife, then took a deep breath when she smiled slightly at him. "We'd like to see you settle down, Kenneth. You're our oldest, and you need to figure out what you're doing with your life."

Kenneth frowned, his handsome features slipping too-easily into the familiar expression. "I know what I'm doing. The firm is successful, my bank account is solid, I have a wonderful family."

Mom's other hand was shaking when she lifted it and made a little move towards Dad. He understood, and leaned forward to take it. Together, they both turned to Kenneth.

"We mean a wife and a family of your own, son," Dad said softly. "Your mother…" He took another deep, painful breath. "She's waiting. She wants to know you're happy, and so do I."

She's waiting.

Kenneth's blue eyes slammed up to Mom's, his expression panicked. "I *am* happy, Mom, I swear."

It was hard to tell how much of her nod was intentional and how much was just part of the constant tremors, but Kenneth seemed to take it as understanding. He slumped back against the couch, his brows drawn in worriedly, as he watched Mom.

One of the pups got too close to the fire, and Mack barked out a command. The suddenness of it seemed to diffuse the tension in the room, and soon they were laughing at the way Kalli was chasing the black pup all over the place.

But Marybeth kept her hand around her mother's, and Kenneth kept glancing thoughtfully at her as well.

It might not be a Merry Christmas for all of them, but it was going to be a Christmas to remember, that was for sure.

You can read exactly *how* Kenneth handles his parents' ultimatum in *Billionaire's Bargain.*

CAIT AND ARCHIE

Cait and Archie
Chasing Change
(Note: the epilogue from Cait and Archie's book—their wedding—took place in February…two months after this short story.)

"I heard from Jack today."

Cait swallowed her shrimp noodles and nodded at Archie, sitting across from her at the small table in one of Bangkok's five-star restaurants on the top floor of their luxury hotel. "Oh really? What did he have to say?"

Archie leaned back in his chair and studied the remains of his dinner. He'd chosen a western-style beef dish for his Christmas Eve fare, while Cait's dish was one of the local specialties.

"He's spending Christmas with his sister in Riston, so I heard all about them. Apparently his niece Nellie has suddenly gotten into acting."

Cait's brows went up as she put down her chopsticks and rested her chin on her palm. "Really? This is Joshua Hardy's kid, right?" Anyone who knew Jaclyn knew Joshua. "I didn't know she was theatrical."

"Jack thinks it might have something to do with a *boy* who's in the local school's theater group."

She chuckled and rolled her eyes. *"Teenagers.* Still, I'm glad he could help."

"Yeah, I think he might be considering sticking around a bit." Archie shrugged. "He hasn't been particularly happy in Hollywood, and I think his sister adopting those kids has affected him. Like he's suddenly got a family."

"Oh!" Cait sat up a bit. "What about—you know, that television show?" It had started being filmed at the ranch before she'd quit her job. "The one about the historical ranch. Could he get a part in that?"

When Archie frowned, she could see the lines around his mouth, now that his beard was neatly trimmed. When they'd met, he'd worn what she'd jokingly called a "mountain man" beard for the role he'd been playing, but now he tended to maintain it better, since he was in between shoots.

"You don't think it's a little stereotypical; the Native American in the cowboy show?"

She shrugged and picked up her chopsticks once more. "I don't think the show was *that* cowboy-y. But yeah, not nearly as many explosions as Jack is used to."

Archie planted his elbows on the table. "Have you been secretly watching Jack Raven action flicks without me?"

Her impish grin was probably answer enough. "I pull them up on my laptop," she whispered conspiratorially, "after I finish one of my favorite Archibald St. John movies."

His return smile was soft, gentle. That's what she loved about him; Archie could be hard and dangerous or soft and thoughtful or any combination of attributes. He *was* all those things, and more. She loved how he was constantly changing, constantly keeping her on her toes.

The last few months, traveling around the world with him, had been the happiest of her life. Only one thing would make her happier, and he hadn't given her any indication he was ready to make a life-long commitment…yet.

"So…" He leaned back in his chair once more, smiling appreciatively at her. "You *haven't* been naughty this year, huh?"

She snorted, then devolved into giggles once more. "Why? Are you keeping track? You're not Santa!"

Archie waggled his eyebrows. But despite his attempt at looking silly, Cait smiled. He was so handsome, backlit by the big picture window and Bangkok lit up below him.

An adventure.

"I'm not Santa, but I wasn't sure if I should give you your present now or tomorrow morning."

She slammed her palm down on the table. "*Archibald St. John*! We agreed we weren't going to exchange presents! You've been *spoiling* me these last few months, taking me all over, showing me everything I've ever wanted to see—"

"*Everything?*"

"Well, almost." She waved her hand dismissively. "I guess we've only seen a fraction of the world. But *still*. We just finished two weeks in an *elephant sanctuary*, Archie! I don't need a *gift*. Not after something like that. And I certainly haven't bought you anything."

She didn't bother to stop her frown as her hands flew through the air in irritation. He couldn't just spring *presents* on her on Christmas Eve, not when she hadn't had the chance to get *him* anything.

But he surprised her.

Rather than sitting there watching her rant, Archie lunged across the table—it was a miracle he didn't spill anything on that suit of his—and grabbed one of her flailing hands in his.

"Cait," he said in a low voice, staring into her eyes. "*Cait.*"

She forced herself to slow down, to take a deep breath. "What?" She scowled.

"Caitlin Quinn, *you* are my gift. Not a day goes by that I don't thank the Lord for putting me in your path. You've accepted me as I am, and have turned out to be the best companion—for life and for traveling—I'd ever hoped to imagine. *You* are my greatest adventure."

Oh.

Oh, that was lovely, wasn't it?

Slowly, Cait relaxed into her chair. Her slight smile was a little sheepish, and she squeezed his hand in return.

"I feel like the last few months have been a dream, honestly," She confessed in a whisper. "I love you so much, and I'm getting to travel around the world with you!"

"I love you too, Cait."

Tomorrow afternoon they had a flight to England, where they'd spend a few days with his mum before flying back to Riston for the new year. It would be nice to see her family again, and she couldn't *wait* to tell her best friend Katie all about their adventures. But for now, it was just her and Archie…and the gorgeous, exciting lightscape of Bangkok spread below them.

Still, she had to be upfront: "I didn't get you anything, because we said we weren't exchanging gifts. Besides, I can't think of anything you don't already own."

He shrugged. "I was thinking about a yacht."

"A *what?*" Her eyes opened wide in shock. "You want me to buy you a *yacht?*"

Archie's chuckle was relaxed. "Nah, I'm thinking about getting *us* a yacht. Wouldn't that be cool? We could use it as our home base, to come back to after our adventures."

She narrowed her eyes. "A yacht. That would certainly be a…a change."

"Yes! Yes." He laughed outright. "I was thinking we could call it *Chasing Change.*"

This time she joined him in his laughter.

Chasing Change would certainly be appropriate.

"I love having adventures with you, Archie."

"I'm glad you say that." His grin turned devious as he reached into his jacket pocket. "Because…" He pulled out what looked like two airline tickets. "Here's your Christmas gift."

When he waggled them at her, she snatched them out of his hand.

"Los Angeles to Nairobi?" she breathed, looking up at him.

His grin was huge. "We leave on safari the second week of January."

A safari! She squealed and grabbed his hand. "Giraffes! Camping on the Serengeti!"

He began to laugh. "Merry Christmas, my love!"

Life was an adventure, indeed!

If you're curious, you can catch up with Jack Raven in *Librarian's Legend!*

OKIE AND NICK

Okie and Nick
Bigfoot Believer

The apartment rang with cheerful voices.

"And since we've no place to go..."

From the kitchen, Jason's baritone joined in. "Let it snow, let it snow, let it snow!"

Lacey screamed with joy and clapped her hands. "Dada! Dada!"

The baby's interruption caused Okie—who was sitting cross-legged beside her—to dissolve into giggles, especially when Nick, who was lying near the tree with his head propped up on Rajah's bulk, blew a raspberry and made little Lacey squeal again.

"Mo'!" the girl shouted. "Mo'!"

But Dink groaned and held up her hands, palm out. "No more, baby girl! Mama can't carry a tune, and Nick isn't participating."

"Mama!"

"Hey now!" Nick rolled over until he could prop his head up on one hand. "I'm humming along. I don't know the words, unlike Miss Smarty Pants over there."

He smiled at Okie, to let her know he was teasing. In the months since they'd realized this deep, fulfilling feeling they felt towards one another was *love*, he'd gotten better at that. And she'd gotten better at reading him.

From the beginning, Nick had been different, as far as Okie was concerned. She knew she was different from everyone around her, but so was he, and he was different in a *good* way. She could understand him, and he could understand her. And they'd developed little ways to make it easier. Like the way he smiled—just slightly—when he was teasing her.

It made her heart light to smile back.

"I can't help it if you have a terrible memory."

"I don't," he groaned. "But who knows the *fourth* verse of *Silent Night*? Who knew there *was* a fourth verse?"

From the kitchen, where he was working on the evening meal, Jason called out, "I do!"

Dink chuckled and thrust herself to her feet. "Of *course* you do! You two deserve one another!" she called over her shoulder to Okie as she headed for the kitchen. "What's taking so long in here?"

"Oh," came Jason's disembodied voice, "have you come to help?"

Dink hummed, then there was silence for a moment, which meant Okie's foster brother and his wife were probably making out. She met Nick's eyes, and this time his smile wasn't coded at all. *This* smile was wide and accompanied by a slight blush.

That's how she knew he was thinking about kissing, the same as her.

Okie was leaning towards him, her lips already parted breathlessly in anticipation, when Lacey screeched for a third time. Nick, whose attention had been solely on Okie's lips, winced slightly, then rolled his eyes. She fell towards him at the same time as little Lacey threw herself at him as well, and the three of them ended up in a tangle beside the Christmas tree.

"Ra!" the baby said, reaching for the huge cat. "RaRa!"

Lacey wasn't even a full year yet, but watching her learn had been a joy of Okie's during the months since she'd come to Riston. Her niece was one smart cookie.

Niece nice Nick nice.

Her mind had been more centered since falling in love with Nick, and for the first time ever, Okie knew what she wanted from her future. She wasn't just drifting anymore, even though she knew that's what Nick thought.

Sometimes she still took off in her truck, driving places to find new vistas to paint. Sometimes she crashed right here in Dink and Jace's living room. And sometimes she stayed in Nick's spare bedroom.

She loved that he didn't want to tie her down, and that he loved her just the way she was. But just the way she was wasn't cutting it anymore.

She watched Nick as he carefully lifted Lacey away from Rajah—who stared imperiously as if he'd expected nothing less—and set her scooting across the room for her push-walker. He was smiling slightly as he watched her go, and Okie pushed herself back up to sit cross-legged in front of him.

"This is nice," she blurted.

But he didn't seem surprised as his gaze flicked back to hers. "It is," he agreed. "I'm glad your brother invited us—he's a much better cook than I am. And being here for Lacey's first Christmas is really special too."

Frustrated at not being able to express herself properly, Okie glanced over to where the baby was pulling herself up on her toy. "I mean… *This*. It's nice. I want this."

"A baby?" Nick blurted, obviously following her gaze to Lacey.

Okie's head swung back around so fast, she probably got whiplash. "*What?* No! No!" She shook her head, then shrugged, then shook it once more. "I mean, yes, maybe one day, but not—no."

Still, she blushed. Until that moment, she'd never thought about being a parent, a mother. But the idea of *maybe* one day having a baby with Nick… that was nice.

And terrifying.

But nice, too.

Kinda.

She took a deep breath. "I meant this. Being here. With you." Her voice dropped to a whisper. "All the time."

Nick sat up, suddenly serious, and reached for her hand. "Okie, you know I love you just as you are. I don't want to ever pressure you into being someone else, and that means I'm not going to ask you to stay."

Squeezing his hand, she raised her eyes from his chin. "I love you too,

Nick," she whispered. "And I *want* to stay. With you. I want this all the time."

Home help hold hands.

"I want to be with you," she finished weakly.

"I would love that, Okie. But…are you sure?"

She *was*. She nodded. "Maybe I could move into your apartment?"

His lips twitched slightly. "I have a better idea. Since Jamal moved out and I've got all that extra space, how about we *both* get a smaller place, one like this, just the two of us? We could put our names on the waiting list."

She frowned. "No. I mean, yes, that is nice, and we can move my paintings and I can pay my way now." Her online shop was taking commissions almost faster than she could paint. "But that's not what I meant."

"What do you mean, then?" he asked softly.

It was always hard to meet someone's eyes. Okie stared at Nick's chin, and tried to explain. "I want…when Jace and Dink see each other, they kiss. They have Lacey. They *know*. They know where they belong and how to get there and that the other one will always be there. They…they're *partners*. I want to be your partner, I think." Her eyes flicked up to his, just briefly. "I love you."

His grip on her hand had tightened until it was almost painful. "Okie," he asked in a strained voice, as if he was holding his breath. "Do you mean…like…*marriage?*"

Marriage.

Marry Merry Nicholas Christmas.

With the refrain running through her head, Okie slowly nodded. "Yes." She exhaled. "Yes, marriage."

She met his eyes, and saw the hope and joy in his dark eyes. He didn't say anything, but didn't loosen his grip either.

"Nick…" She took a deep breath. "Will you marry me?"

His breath exploded out of him as a huge smile lit up his face. Leaning forward, he gathered her in his arms—awkward, since they were both sitting on the floor—and pressed his cheek to hers.

"Okie, I would love nothing more."

"Are you sure?" she asked, doubting herself suddenly. "I know it's not normal—"

But he cut her off. "I've been in love with my best friend for ages, Okie. Of *course* I want to spend the rest of my life with you, being surprised by the way you think. *I love you.*"

Pressed against him, she smiled. "I love you too," she whispered.

"How about we go down to the judge on Wednesday, and see about getting the paperwork started?"

Marriage paperwork. "That sounds like a good idea."

She felt him smile.

"Thank you for making this the best Christmas ever, Okie."

"I think you'd better kiss me, before we have to go help my niece with her walking."

So he did.

Marry Merry Nicholas Christmas!

***

See the bonus material at the end of this collection to read how Lacey first came into Dink and Jace's lives!

LIN AND BRANDON

Lin and Brandon
Finding Fortune

Brandon held the door open for her with a smile, and as always, Lin's face heated as she glanced at her handsome husband's profile. In the months they've been married, she kept hoping maybe her reaction to him would calm down a bit, and she could quit blaming it on the warmth of the kitchen…but no.

And as she smiled back, she had to admit she didn't mind *that* much.

Hopefully he'll still make me feel this way when we're as old as Mr. Lee!

Speaking of which… "Are you sure Mr. Lee is okay to close down the restaurant tonight?"

Brandon clucked at her as they entered the back room of the Riston Food Bank, their arms full of containers. "Stop worrying! He's old, not decrepit!"

She had to giggle at his impression of their mentor, who'd taken on a much less-stressful role at *The Golden Fortune* restaurant since Brandon had come on board as a chef. Mr. Lee still cooked, but he wasn't usually there from opening 'til closing, like he was today.

Her husband nudged her with his hip. "Hey, I mean it," he said in a soft voice. When she glanced at him, he winked. "He'll be okay. We can stop by on the way back to the apartment, if you want."

Sighing, Lin bit her lip. "Maybe…" She had other plans for tonight, plans which included the steak and potatoes in the fridge at home, some mistletoe, and a pregnancy test…

Just not all at once. That would be gross.

"Merry Christmas, Ms. Lin!"

Sean Shulman's cheerful yell distracted Lin from her nervous musings. The boy—teenager, really—waved to them from behind the counter where he was helping to organize and load boxes.

Brandon jerked his chin at their young friend. "Merry Christmas Eve, Sean! Here's the lo mein and chicken fried rice, as promised. Where do you want it?"

"Um, put it here." The boy pointed at the counter. "And I'll go tell Mom it's here."

He ducked through one of the doors while Brandon unloaded his boxes and helped Lin stack hers beside them. She breathed a sigh of relief —although the carry-out wasn't really that heavy—and rubbed her lower back surreptitiously.

Sean's mother Heather backed in through the door, calling through it, "And find a new pair of gloves, Sophie!" She was shaking her head when she met Lin's eyes. "That girl, I swear. I don't know how she manages to get so *dirty*."

Lin smiled in return, but knew hers was probably thoughtful. What would her child be like? Both she and Brandon had the straight black hair and eye-shape of their Chinese ancestors, but Lin's eyes were green. That's what Brandon had noticed first, what had first brought them together. Whoever their child took after, would he or she have her work ethic, or Brandon's ability to whip up a full dinner in a matter of minutes? Or would he or she end up more like Sophie; rambunctious and wild?

Luckily, Heather hadn't noticed Lin's daydreaming, and was already instructing Brandon where to unpack the food she and her kids would be packaging for the local shelters and churches. Sean jumped right in to help, and Lin couldn't help but be impressed by the boy's willingness to work for others…especially mid-afternoon on Christmas Eve!

She'd only met him once before, when he brought a date—what had her name been?—into the restaurant. He'd been polite and considerate, and even Lin could see the girl had been impressed. Whoever she was, she'd probably be even more impressed to see him now!

"So, got any big plans for tonight?" Brandon was asking the Shumans.

Sean shrugged. "We always do Christmas Eve games at Uncle Andrew's house. This year he's bringing Rachel, which is cool. I like her."

His mother inserted herself into the conversation. "I do too. And we have some high hopes for this evening." Her exaggerated wink made her son scoff. "I know for a fact he's put up some mistletoe, and has been saving money."

Andrew McIver was going to *propose*? Lin's eyes widened. She knew the engineer—he'd come into *The Golden Fortune* on dates quite often, including last month with a cute Indian woman. That had to be the lady—Rachel—Heather was talking about.

Her son didn't seem to understand though. "What does that have to do with anything?"

Brandon chuckled. "I think you'll find out soon, buddy. How was your December?" he asked, changing the subject.

Sean shrugged, his attention on the boxes of food. "It was alright. We went to Quinn Valley and hung out with Mom's family, so that was pretty cool. I met a lot of people."

"Yeah." Brandon's dark gaze flicked to Heather just briefly. "Don't you have a cousin?"

"Jer. He's little, but he thinks I'm cool, so that's cool."

Lin didn't know the full story of why Heather had been estranged from her family for so long, but it was good to hear they were making amends.

"Family is important," she said softly, her palms resting on her stomach under her sweater. She'd left her jacket in the car, figuring it wasn't too far to go with the food.

"Speaking of which…" Heather's smile was kind as she raked Lin with her green gaze. "You're looking great. Congratulations!"

"Thank y—" The appreciation was instinctual, until Lin's brain caught up with Heather's words and she snapped her mouth shut on a massive blush.

Brandon noticed—of course he did—and immediately turned to her. "What?" He was obviously confused, and he would be.

Lin tried another smile for Heather, but it came out weak and awkward. "Thank you," she managed this time, hoping Brandon would drop the subject.

He didn't. Instead, he reached for her hand. "Lin? What's wrong?"

"Nothing's wrong, she just said I look great."

"Of course you do, but what…"

He trailed off just as Heather gasped hugely and slapped her forehead.

"*Oh my gosh.* Oh my gosh, did I just let the cat out of the bag? *Oh my gosh I'm so sorry!*"

Heather backed away from the couple and the counter, shaking her head. "I didn't even think, Lin, I'm so sorry! I've just— I'm one of the only single teachers at the school, you know? I just—I can tell when one of our ladies is expecting, you're glowing, and I didn't think— I'm so sorry!"

She grabbed Sean's arm and began pulling him back towards the door she'd originally entered through. "We'll just go and— You can have some time—I'm sorry!" As the door swung shut behind them, she called out, "Merry Christmas!"

The sudden silence stretched, and Lin was sure Brandon was holding his breath as much as she was. She stared at the door, wondering if she should brush off Heather's words and pretend nothing had happened, so she could go on with the big reveal that evening.

"Lin?" her husband asked softly. "What did she— Did all that mean what I think it meant?"

She winced and turned to Brandon, who was looking at her with such a hopeful expression she couldn't bear the thought of disappointing him. After all, she could lie to him.

"Lin?" he repeated, a little more forcefully. His hand was warm in hers as he tugged her around to face him. "Are you…?"

She sighed, rolled her eyes, and gave in to the inevitable. "We're going to have a baby."

His whoop was loud enough to echo in the loading room, as he wrapped his arms around her and swept her in a circle. "A baby! *Yes!*" Then he froze in place and gently lowered her to the ground. "Wait, I shouldn't— Are you okay? I shouldn't have manhandled you—"

Her laughter interrupted him. "I don't mind your manhandling, *husband.*"

"Lin," he breathed, grabbing each of her cheeks in his palms. "A *baby.*"

She smiled at the wonder in his expression. "I'm only about six weeks along, but I guess that's enough for *some* people to tell." She had to chuckle then at Heather's awkwardness. "I had a big plan to tell you tonight. A nice meal, and I have the test wrapped up like a present."

Brandon opened his mouth to say something, then closed it, then opened it again. It was like he couldn't decide what to say, how to react, and suddenly, Lin burst into giggles and wrapped her arms around his neck.

"I had everything planned out, but *this* was exactly what I was hoping for."

"What? For someone else to figure it out before your dolt of a husband?"

"No, silly!" She was still smiling hugely. "Your reaction. I wish I'd been recording it."

"We're going to have a *baby*, Lin." His hands rested against her back. "I wonder if she'll have your eyes."

His thoughts were so similar to hers that Lin had to giggle again. "I wonder what Mr. Lee is going to say."

"Year of the Earth Pig is very successful year to be born in," Brandon said in the voice he used to mimic the old man's. "Very good choice."

She laughed in earnest then, then reached up to kiss him. "I love you, husband."

"I love you too." His lips brushed against hers. "Thank you for the most wonderful Christmas present ever!"

You've met the Shulmans before, but Heather will finally get her spotlight in *Librarian's Legend!*

BONUS: DINK AND JACE'S ADOPTION STORY

Bonus: Dink and Jace's adoption story
*This story has previously only been published on my website for my newsletter subscribers. But now you get to experience this very special catch-up as well! This is **not** a Christmas story.*
Click here to find Wild West Wedding

"You wanna head to trivia tonight?"

Dink looked up from their tiny kitchen table, where she'd been staring out the window and nursing her coffee. For the last three hours. Since last fall, when the doctor had given them the news, she'd done this more and more.

"Hmmm?" she asked her husband, not sure if he'd said anything more and she'd just been too flaked out to hear him.

Jace's handsome face softened. He stood by the front door to the tiny house they'd been renting for almost a year and a half, still bundled up in his winter gear. He held a handful of mail in one hand—they got all their mail directed to his accounting office here at River's End Ranch—and was peeling off his scarf with the other.

Not for the first time, Dink wondered how someone as tall as her husband could manage to be comfortable in this tiny house. As it was, sitting at the kitchen table, she could reach out and touch him, standing at the front door. But they'd learned to manage, and it was *fun*. Besides, it was just the two of them.

Would only ever *be* just the two of them…

"I asked," Jace repeated gently, "if you wanted to go to trivia tonight. We haven't been in a while, and I recall you and I made a pretty good team."

Dink snorted. "*I* recall you didn't think I had anything to offer, Mr. Smarty-Pants."

"You're remembering incorrectly," Jace deadpanned, slotting the mail into the appropriate "bills to be addressed" or "wastebasket" piles.

She lifted her coffee to sip, but it'd long since gone cold. "Did you just call me wrong?"

"I did!" Jace nodded too enthusiastically to be anything but teasing. "*That's* the word I was looking for."

A grin reluctantly pulled at Dink's lips. How long had it been since she'd let herself go and really laughed? She and Jace were so very different, but they'd made the perfect odd couple, and were so good together.

It wasn't until their infertility diagnosis that things had gotten choppy. After researching extensively, they'd decided not to tackle IVF—in-vitro fertilization—because of the strain it would cause on Dink, their savings, and their relationship…and because the doctor said there was a low likelihood of it working. Jace had made his peace with not having biological children, but there were days like today—beautiful winter days where the snow was just *begging* to be played in—that Dink couldn't concentrate on her sewing, for all the obsessing she was doing over what it would be like to have a child.

"Hey, hon."

Dink must've been quieter longer than she'd intended, because Jace stepped up behind her and rubbed his large hand down her back. She hummed in question, pretending she didn't know what he was going to scold her about, and started gathering up her coffee mug and the napkin with the cookie crumbs scattered across it.

But he didn't scold her for getting dreamy, or remind her they'd made the decision together. Instead, he dropped a kiss to her head. "I love you, Dink."

She twisted in her chair and wrapped her arms around his waist, although she had to stretch up to do so. "I love you too," she muttered against his jacket.

"So let's get you bundled up, and go get some pizza, eh? I'll bet we can kick Jaclyn and Simon's team's butt."

She played along, knowing the only way to feel better was to pretend to feel better. *Fake it 'til you make it.* "I think, since there's so many of them, the correct term is *butts*, husband."

"See?" He knocked her with his hip. "This is why I need you on my team."

Pizza *did* sound good, even if it was a little early. "I'll get my new scarf."

"And I'll get mine." He'd left it hanging at home, since he claimed it clashed with his boring gray overcoat.

In December, Jace had asked Dink to teach him to knit so they could knit each other Christmas presents. The request had been out of left field, and she'd been totally shocked. After all, her husband was a no-nonsense, straight-laced accountant...not at all the artsy type.

It wasn't until their second lesson—curled up together on their tiny couch—that Dink had realized the truth: Jace had asked not because he cared about the outcome, but because he'd wanted to spend time with her. The request, and their subsequent knitting sessions, had been her favorite Christmas present of the year.

So now she got her lumpy, lopsided beige scarf from its peg by the door...and Jace got his beautiful lime-green-and-lavender one too. And they smiled as they each wrapped up tight.

Her life might not be going exactly where she'd planned, but it was still pretty awesome.

Impulsively, she stretched up on her tip-toes to kiss him quickly. "I love you."

"You do?" He frowned. "Are you sure?"

Her eyes widened. Had she done something to make him think otherwise? She'd been in a funk recently, but she *always* made sure he knew how much she appreciated his love and support. "Of course I do!"

"Hmmm." He put his arms around her and pulled her closer. "Then you really should kiss me…" Leaning closer, he lowered his voice. "Like this."

Dink hummed in agreement when his lips caressed hers, and wrapped her own arms around his middle—the highest she could reach. Even though they were both bundled up, she could feel his warmth and his touch.

She loved him so much.

"So, pizza?" he asked when they finally pulled apart.

"Pizza," she agreed.

He was pulling open the door when his phone rang loudly in his pocket, so he shut it again quickly. "Sorry." He pulled it out and checked the number. "It's not five o'clock. Could be the office, but I don't recognize the number."

"Go ahead." Dink nodded with a smile.

He clicked the green *answer* button. "Hello? Yes, this is Jace."

Her husband's eyes slowly round. "Wait, hold on. I'm going to put you on speaker. Dink's here."

He clicked the button, and held up the phone. "It's Peggy, the social worker. Go ahead, Peggy."

In the moment between the first sentence and the next, Dink's heart seized up. Why was Peggy calling? Was it good news? They'd had their share of disappointments over the last few months, as potential adoptions had fallen through. Their preference was to adopt a baby, but there were so many being born with chemical dependencies and issues, it'd been nearly heartbreaking to decide what was best.

"Can you both hear me?" Peggy asked.

Dink's throat had closed up, so she just nodded, even knowing the other woman couldn't hear her. Thank goodness Jace was calm enough to say, "Yes, we can." He fumbled for her hand, and Dink clasped it like a life-line, even through two layers of gloves.

"Okay, you two. I know we've been through your limits of what kind of dependencies you're willing to take in an infant. You said a non-smoker mother, so I need to ask you again: Are you okay with a mother who smoked occasionally during her second and third trimester?"

"Um…hold on." Jace pressed the phone against his thigh, so Peggy wouldn't be able to hear their conversation. "What do you think?" He asked Dink.

She just blinked up at him, not quite following this. Peggy was asking…*what,* exactly?

"Dink!" he prompted. "Are we okay with take a baby whose biological mother smoked occasionally?"

"Are we?" she whispered.

He took a deep breath, then let it out slowly. "I am. I'd obviously prefer no foreign substances during pregnancy, but that's going to be hard to find. I think we should just say yes, so we can increase our chances of being matched with a baby."

A baby. "Then yes," Dink whispered. "I agree with you."

His hold on her hand tightened, if that was possible, and he lifted the phone once more. "You still there, Peggy?"

"Yep. Did you discuss?"

"Yes." He inhaled again. "We agree, as long as the tobacco use was only occasional."

"Excellent." Peggy sounded as if she was checking boxes. "And you said you were okay with a baby of mixed race, right?"

Dink snorted softly and offered Jace a watery smile. Her husband was not only biracial himself, he was a graduate of the state's foster system. "Yes," she said. "We most definitely are."

"Okaaay…" It sounded like she was making more notes. "And you've passed all of the tests you need on this end. You think you could stop by the store and grab a carseat on your way to the hospital?"

Dink's gaze slammed into Jace's. His dark skin had gone pale in shock, and she imagined she looked much the same. Her heart was pounding in her ears so loud she didn't think she'd be able to hear anything Peggy said anyhow, but she had to ask…

"Why?" Her strangled whisper wasn't loud enough, but Jace repeated it.

"*Why?*" He asked into the phone.

There was a pause, and Dink stared into her husband's eyes as a calm settled over both of them—over the whole house, the whole world.

"Because," Peggy said lightly over the phone, "Your daughter was born yesterday, and is ready to meet you."

There was probably some screaming, and yelling, and Dink definitely did some jumping up and down after the initial shock wore off. Thank goodness Jace was level-headed enough to take notes on everything they needed to know, because Dink didn't think she could concentrate on anything longer than a moment.

A baby. They were going to meet their daughter. A *daughter*. Her eyes filled with tears. *Their* daughter. As Jace hung up the phone, she grabbed him around the middle.

"A daughter," he whispered, and she could tell from the way his voice caught he was close to tears.

"We're going to have a baby, Jace."

He squeezed her. "Yeah, we are. A *baby*."

They stood in silence for a long moment. All sorts of thoughts were running through her head. *A bed for the baby. A changing pad, diapers, and wipes. Some infant layette, at least until Muz and Ellie can go buy tiny little girl clothes—and I know they will. What else do we need ASAP? Oh, formula and bottles, duh! Where are we going to put all this stuff? We're going to need to look into larger apartments in town I guess...*

It wasn't until she noticed Jace's silence that she stopped to wonder if *he* was thinking the same thoughts. "What're you thinking about?"

His light brown eyes opened and he stared down at her. A rare smile curved his wide lips upwards. "A baby, huh? I'm going to be a daddy."

I'm going to be a mommy. Wow. "Are you happy?"

He squeezed. "Only time I've been happier is that day—right here in this room—you agreed to marry me because I gave you those ridiculous boots!" They both chuckled at the memory. "Only…"

"Only, what?"

"Only…" He dropped a kiss on her forehead. "Only, this isn't at all how I imagined my evening going!"

Laughing, she tugged him towards the front door once more. "This is better than trivia! Let's go buy a carseat! And diapers. And some formula…"

If you've enjoyed these short catch-ups with your favorite characters, I urge you to friend me on Facebook or follow me on Twitter. I frequently post fun stories, links to great books, and cute animal pictures.
If you'd like to keep up with my books, read deleted scenes, or receive exclusive free books, sign up for my newsletter.

And if newsletters aren't your thing, come join my reader group, Caroline's Cohort!

If you love the world we've created on River's End Ranch, then come play with us in our Quinn Valley Ranch Readers Facebook group, where we chat about the books, behind-the-scenes fun, and contests! And if you're a fan of contemporary western romance in general, we've got a Facebook group for that too!

Please consider leaving a review—it's bread and butter to an author like me!

ACKNOWLEDGMENTS

If you've enjoyed these Christmas epilogues, I urge you to friend me on Facebook or follow me on Twitter. I frequently post fun stories, links to great books, and cute animal pictures.
If you'd like to keep up with my books, read deleted scenes, or receive exclusive free books, sign up for my newsletter.

If you love the world we've created on River's End Ranch, then come play with us in our River's End Ranch Readers Facebook group, where we chat about the books, behind-the-scenes fun, and contests! And if you're a fan of contemporary western romance in general, we've got a Facebook group for that too!

Back in May of 2016 I had the utter pleasure of meeting Kirsten Osbourne, Pamela Kelley, and Cindy Caldwell in Chicago during a conference. Soon after, they invited me to be part of this delightful world they were creating, and introduced me to the wonderful Amelia Adams. I was thrilled to join their team, and have had hours and hours of fun, playing via our imaginations at River's End Ranch.

Thank you, ladies, for letting me be a part of the magic.

And thank you to Alyssa, to my beta readers and Cohort members, to our continuity reader Amy, and to CM Wright, my awesome editor.

Calendar Girls' Ranch (6 books)

Click **here** to find a complete list of Caroline's books.

*Sign up for Caroline's Newsletter to receive exclusive content and freebies, as well as first dibs on her books! Or if newsletters aren't your thing, follow her on **Bookbub** for a quick, concise new release alert every time she publishes a book!*